T0196236

One Night Changed My Life

Also By LaTonia Harrell

You Can Make It, The Enemy's Time Is Up

One Night Changed My Life

LaTonia Harrell

iUniverse, Inc.
New York   Bloomington

One Night Changed My Life

iUniverse books may be ordered through booksellers or by contacting:

iUniverse
1663 Liberty Drive
Bloomington, IN 47403
www.iuniverse.com
1-800-Authors (1-800-288-4677)

ISBN: 978-1-4502-7500-2 (sc)
ISBN: 978-1-4502-7501-9 (ebk)

Printed in the United States of America

iUniverse rev. date: 11/9/2010

Dedication

This book is dedicated to the world. My prayer is that we all take heed to the Enemy's tricks—and trust me, there are many. He comes to steal, kill, and destroy. He's no amateur; he's the master of his games. Let's get back to the basics—the Bible, morals, values, family, self-respect, self-worth, and love for one another.

I also dedicate this book to my brother. We didn't have a lot of time together, but I'll cherish every conversation we had forever. Melvin D. Williams was someone that believed in me and looked forward to reading the book. Sad to say, his life was taken in 2009 at the age of twenty-nine by a bullet before the book was released. See, one of the tricks of the Enemy … violence and hatred among one another.

Last but not least, to the woman who was like an aunt to me. She loved me like an auntie should love her niece. She was big on God, love, family, and self-respect. She was so excited and couldn't wait to get this book in her hands. During the last conversation we had about the book, she said, "Tonia, from the time I've known you, over eighteen years, I've always seen greatness in you. There is nothing you can't accomplish. Keep God first and follow his lead. Your book is sure to make a difference in the life of each person that reads it." Auntie Sherry Lee Hill went home to be with the Lord in 2009; she will forever be in my heart. To my entire Princesses in True Girlfriends, this one is for you. Stay rooted in God, and at all times remember that your body is a *temple*.

It only takes one time for something to happen in your life that can cause it to be turned upside down. Every choice you make in life has consequences.

—LaTonia Harrell

Acknowledgments

First and foremost, I would like to give all glory and honor to God. Truly, I'm thankful for his grace and mercy.

Secondly, I am blessed to have a loving and supportive husband, James, who encourages me to do every assignment God gives me. I love you, baby. I thank God for you.

Thirdly, I want to thank my children, Audrey, Joshua, Taneah, Kalyn, and James, for all of the love and support they give.

Finally, I want to thank all of the people who believe in me and prayed for me along the way.

To my mother, evangelist Denise Davis—thanks for all of the love and support you give. Truly, I'm blessed to have you as a mother. There's not a day that goes by that I don't lift my hands and say, "Thank you, Lord, for my mother."

To my spiritual mother, author La Veeta Ivory—words can't express the love and respect I have for you. Thank you for all of your love, support, and guidance throughout the years. Your ministry is such a blessing to me. Those interested in learning more about LaVeeta's ministry may visit http://www.laveetaivory.com.

To my grandmothers, Mother Rether Jordan and Ann Williams. I love you both so very much.

I want to express my deepest appreciation and love to Pastors Ernest and Emma Tillman, two amazing, anointed leaders. I thank God for Family Praise and Worship Ministry—a ministry that stands firm on the Word of God.

Dr. Kelly Tucker, thanks for all of your support.

Many thanks also to Mother Alvina Rhinehart, Tuesdai Noelle, Sydney Lauren Ivory, Mrs. Keisha Hines, Jermaine Jackson, Coach Rabbit, a.k.a. "Aunt BB," the Sisters Building Sisters Worldwide Ministries & True Girlfriends, Jose and Hillary Santos, Jermaine and Nadia Lawton, and Aunt Dean, a.k.a. "Markie."

Special thanks to cover designer Mr. Keith Saunders at http://www.mariondesigns.com, Ms. Gina B. Flagg, Lil Greg "Fathead," Dante, Satina, and Gregory T. Williams.

I love you, Uncle Brah, a.k.a. "Mark Taylor," Uncle Freddie, Titus, and author Raymond Blalock.

Introduction

What kind of woman of God would I be if I didn't try to catch as many as I can before they fall into the very thing that might change their lives forever? The Enemy is a thief. He comes to kill, steal, and destroy whomever he can, however he can. Your age, race, or gender doesn't matter to him. He wants you, and he wants you badly. He doesn't care if you come from the hood or the suburbs. He's a deceiver; he makes things look good. You know the saying "Trick or Treat"? Well, please believe me, the Enemy is never coming to give you a good treat—it's a trick.

See, we live in a world today where it's all about the look and pretty much nothing else. There is a lack of self-respect and self-worth. For some, morals and values are out the door. Material things and what looks good are in, and nothing else matters.

When God gave me the title *One Night Changed My Life,* I thought, "Okay, Lord, where are we going with this?" After two days with God, and after typing up all that he was saying to me, the tears fell. I was so touched by this. I began to worship and praise God like never before, because this could have been me, you, or one of our loved ones. Thank God for his grace and his mercy.

Pretty is the name that God gave me for the young lady in the story. See, that's all it takes for some and just a little more for others—for a fly, fine guy to say, "Hi, pretty." Now, don't get me wrong—men need to be aware, too. Everything that looks good isn't good for you, either. Sit back and take a look inside the life of a young, beautiful, gifted, and talented young lady who was destined for greatness as she tells her story of how one night changed her life.

Chapter 1

My name is Pretty. You see, my mom always warned me about that. She said, "Never let your name go to your head. And remember that your body is a temple." Did I listen? Of course not, but I sure wish that I had. It's been said that no one can tell your life story better than you can. So sit back and let me tell you how one night changed my life …

Pretty as can be with my Coca-Cola shape, I was so fly, and yes, still a virgin. I had just graduated from Madison High School in Milwaukee and was ready for a night of celebration. While driving home from graduation with a few of my homegirls, we decided to stop and get a bite to eat from McDonald's on Capitol. See, Capitol Drive is the spot. That's where all of the fly guys hang out. You know, the guys with the candy paint, the ballers with the Benzes, Lexuses, and of course the SUVs sitting on twenty-fours.

"Well, here we are." I smiled. "The hot spot—Mickey D's. We made it, ladies, and it's on and popping in the parking lot."

My homegirls and I were so excited. All around us was money, money, money. Before getting out of the car to get our walk on and come up with each baller that we could, we rushed and got the Mac lip gloss out to prepare to blow the minds of those who set their eyes on us. Before opening the car door, I looked at all of my homegirls and told them, "We're so beautiful, and any man that gets a conversation from us is considered lucky." We all clapped five and said, "Let's do it."

All four of the doors opened at once, and all you could hear was the rap music bumping from Lil Wayne. We all said, "Hey … that's our song!" We looked at one another and said, "Walk time!" See, "walk time" means that you go your way, and I go my way, and we meet back up in fifteen minutes in the spot where we started. We hugged one another and said, "Be safe," and "Be sure to pick a winner." See, we were a fly clique. We had class and order about ourselves.

I walked in the direction of this candy-red Benz sitting on twenty-twos with a license plate that had "Why Not?" on it, straight from Florida. So I walked past, and I heard this fly guy say, "Excuse me, pretty. What's your name?" I acted like I didn't hear him. I didn't want to seem too easy.

Again, he said, "Excuse me, pretty …" elevating his voice that time.

"How do you know my name?" I asked, stepping back a little as he stepped toward me.

"Baby, I don't," he said as he smiled, checking me out from head to toe. "But I'd love to know your name and get to know you."

"Oh, really? Somehow I think you know my name. You called it two times already."

He laughed. "Oh, you one of those stuck-up chicks. The ones that like to play hard to get."

"Anything worth having is worth working hard for, correct?"

"Yes, baby, I agree."

He stepped closer, and I didn't step back. All I could see standing before me was a man with a million-dollar smile ... a fine and fly brother from Florida.

"Now that we did the back-and-forth thing, what's your name, pretty?"

"You got it." I smiled. "You answered your own question. It's Pretty. What's yours?"

He laughed. "You got jokes. Anyways, my name is Nehemiah."

I said, "Nehemiah ... that's nice. It's also a biblical name."

"Yeah, I know. You must go to church to know that my name is biblical."

"Yes, sir, every Sunday. What about you?" I asked, knowing the answer already.

He said, "Sunday service and Wednesday Bible studies."

I laughed and said, "Baby, please, you a baller. You hit the streets 24–7."

He said, "Baby, I work two jobs to afford what I have. Nothing comes to me easy. I punch a clock every day to keep my money right. I work hard, baby. Please believe that."

I said, "Oh, really, Nehemiah? Well, good for you. It was nice talking to you. I got to go."

He said, "Can I get your name, at least?"

"I told you. My name is Pretty."

Still smiling, he said, "Take my number. Maybe I can take you out tonight since it's your graduation night."

I said, "How do you know that it's my graduation night?"

He said, "Your homegirl still has on her cap and gown."

"Oh, yeah," I said, laughing.

He then said, "I might even buy you an outfit to wear as a gift."

"A gift?" I said. "Oh, really, N."

He said, "What?"

I said, "Baby, your name is too long, so I'll just call you by your first initial, N."

He said, "You a mess and something else."

I said, "And you know it. Give me your number. I may call, may not. I've already given you too much conversation."

We both smiled as I walked away. I was late for the fifteen-minute meet-up that my homegirls and I have after walk time. I didn't want them to worry, so I power walked all the way back to the meet-up spot, about to fall out in my four-inch heels.

Once I reached the spot, all of my homegirls said, "Pretty, we were worried. You're never late for the meet-up."

I said, "Girls, I met a winner!"

They said, "Girl, please … who and where?"

We all laughed, and they moved in closer to hear the details.

"Here and now," I said. "He's from Florida … fly, fine, and has a million-dollar smile. His name is Nehemiah."

They said, "What?"

I said, "N. Just call him N. He gave me his number and even said that he'd love to take me out and grab me a fit for my graduation gift."

My homegirl Mia said, "He sounds like a winner to me."

So we all laughed, and they started talking about the fly guys they'd met. We loaded into the 2009 Lexus that my grandfather gave me for doing well in school and walking across the stage. I was the first one in the family to graduate from high school on my father's side, so the family went all out for me. As I left Mickey D's, I drove past "Mr. N.," and I stopped and asked, "What time is good for you?"

He said, "Whenever you call is good. I'll make time for you."

"Oh, really?" I said, sipping the remaining Hi-C I'd bought earlier.

"Call and see." He winked, flashing that million-dollar smile.

"I'll do just that," I said, placing the drink back into the cup holder. "These are my homegirls—Mia, Kim, and Maya. I love them like sisters."

He said, "Nice to meet you all. Now what about your name?"

I said, "Kim, please tell him what my name is."

"Her name is Pretty," she said, sticking her head out of the air-conditioned ride.

"Oh, okay," N. said as if he didn't believe her, either.

My girls laughed.

"Well, be expecting my call," I said with a smile.

"Sure will, *Pretty*."

He laughed as we pulled off, and my homegirls started screaming and saying, "Go 'head, girl, he is fine … and his teeth are pearly white with a smile out of this world."

"I told y'all."

Mia said, "Are you going to call him?"

I looked at her and said, "Now, Mia, you know better than that. Of course!"

And we all laughed as I drove down Capitol headed toward Lake Drive, where we all lived, listening to Keyshia Cole. Finally, I dropped my last homegirl Maya off. I was a block away from home. I was tired and wanted a nap before the night started for me. I walked in the house and kissed my parents and sister and said, "Hi, and thanks for the balloons and all the gifts, but I'm going out tonight, and I need a nap. I will talk with you all once I wake up." While walking up the stairs, I yelled, "Oh, yeah, Mom and Dad, I met this nice guy from Florida named Nehemiah."

"Is he a Christian?" they asked. I could feel them looking at each other and wanting me to come back downstairs to discuss it.

"Uh … he goes to church," I hollered while kicking my four-inch heels off. "Does that make him a Christian?"

I closed the door before they had a chance to respond, took off my clothes, put on a pair of shorts and a long T-shirt, and lay down. I grabbed N.'s number to call, but I started thinking that I didn't want to seem too anxious to get with him. Then I thought about the free new outfit that I could get. I said to myself, "He seems cool … why not call?"

I laughed, remembering that it was exactly what his license plate said. "Why not?" I called the number, and his voicemail said, "Pretty, I knew you'd call. Please leave a number where I can reach you, and also leave your real name." I screamed and hung up and called my homegirls on the three-way, saying, "Listen to N.'s voicemail." You know how some girls do when a guy leaves a personal message … they think that there's nobody else. I was thinking maybe, just maybe, he may be the one.

After hanging up with the girls, I called back and left a message saying, "Hi, N., this is Pretty. I'm open and available for a short time tonight. Please feel free to call if you would like to be a man of your word—meaning that you will show me a night on the town and grab me a fly fit. Just kidding. Give me a call. Once again, it's me, Pretty, the one you met at McDonald's today."

About five minutes later, my cell rang, and it was him. I answered the phone in my sexiest voice, saying, "Hello, Pretty speaking. How may I help you?"

He laughed and said, "Wow! You weren't joking; your name is really Pretty. I see the name on my caller ID— Ms. Pretty Jones."

"That's right … I'm Pretty," I said, rolling over onto my back. "What's up?"

"Well, pretty lady, how about eight tonight—we do dinner and a movie? I could drop you off some cash for an outfit as promised, or you can trust me to find you something that will look great on you."

"Well, N., I'm sure you wouldn't know what to get me. It's hard shopping for me. I'm picky."

"Pretty, I seen you today, baby. I got this. Plus I have five sisters, and I buy them gifts all the time and send them back home."

"Cool," I said, holding back a yawn. "Go right ahead." I was tired and needed a nap if I was going to look my best and be on my best behavior. You know how we get when we haven't had enough rest—attitude is off the chain.

"Okay, N.," I said, turning onto my side. "I'll trust your judgment on a fly outfit only because you were fly from head to toe today. I wear a size twelve. You figure out the rest."

He said, "I already knew that."

I laughed. "Boy, please. How will I get the outfit from you?"

"We can meet up once I get it. Or you can come and dress at the hotel where I have a room for the weekend."

I thought, "Hotel? Room for the weekend?"

"You're kidding me, right?" I said, flipping over onto my stomach. "N., you got the wrong one. I'm a virgin and will never lay down with anyone that is not my husband. My mother told me that my body is a temple, and I have to treat it with the utmost respect."

N. said, "Baby, I'm also a virgin, and I feel my body is a temple, as well. The hotel room is for nothing like that. Pretty, I'm being honest with you. But, if it makes you feel better, I'll meet you somewhere to give you the gift."

I said, "Okay, that sounds much better. Hit me up when you're ready to meet."

He said, "Sure thing, baby."

I smiled as I hung up the phone. His voice was so smooth. All I could think about was that million-dollar smile.

The phone rang about two hours later. It was N., saying, "Okay, where you at, and how do I get there? I'm not from Milwaukee, so I'm not too familiar with the streets."

I said, "Do you know where Bayshore Town Center is?"

He said, "Sure do. Me and my boys went to dinner last week over there."

"Meet me in front of the store called Bath & Body Works," I said as I picked my keys up off the bed.

He said, "Okay."

I told him, "Give me twenty minutes, and I will be there. And I'm bringing my dad with me."

He laughed and said, "Cool."

I screamed as I hung up the phone. I thought, "Oh, wow, he is a man of his word." I yelled for my dad to come to my room.

He said, "What's wrong?"

I said, "Dad, come with me to pick up something."

"Something?" he said, raising his eyebrows. "What is it?"

I smiled, patting him on the back. "Come on, Dad. It's a gift from a friend, and I don't want to go by myself."

He said, "It better not be a man buying you anything, Pretty. We have had this talk many times before."

I'm spoiled, so I knew that he would come. All I had to do was say, "*Please,* Daddy."

"Okay. Give me ten minutes."

So, while waiting for my dad, I called all of my homegirls to share the good news. Then my friend Kim asked me, "What did you say his name was again?"

I told her, "Nehemiah. Why?"

She said, "Oh, I was making sure his name wasn't Tony."

I said, "Why?"

Kim paused. "Don't worry about it. It isn't him."

"Okay," I said, still wondering what she was hinting at. "I will call you all once me and my dad get back."

Daddy and I pulled off shortly after I hung up with my homegirls. While driving down to the strip mall, I made my dad listen to the whole Keyshia Cole CD. He was not into the CD at all. He loves the Lord, and gospel music is his only music.

Okay, by then, I was nervous. We were a minute away from the store where I'd told N. to meet me. I thought, "Okay, breathe." My dad looked at me like I was crazy. He said, "Girl, what is wrong with you?"

"Dad, I want you to meet the gentleman I met today at McDonald's," I said, hoping that my dad would somehow be all right with it.

"Pretty, I know you have not brought me here for this," he said sternly.

"*Please,* Dad … and be nice."

Lord have mercy, when I pulled up, N. had a bag in his hand and at least four dozen roses, all colors. I thought, "Oh, my goodness." My dad looked at me in disbelief. I should have left Daddy at home. I parked and got out.

"Hi, Pretty." N. smiled, handing me the roses. "Congratulations for graduating from high school. The best is yet to come."

I said, "Oh, my, you are such a gentleman. And you have great taste."

I looked in the bag, and he had something from Florida for me. He said that it came from his sister's boutique. He brought a bunch of things from his sister's boutique with him to Milwaukee. The dress was beautiful, and I could tell that it was expensive from the material. I didn't want to ask the price; that would've been out of order. So I thanked him and said, "N., I want you to meet my father, Mr. Jones."

N. shook my dad's hand and said that it was an honor to meet the man that brought this pretty young lady into the world. Dad said, "Thanks," and got back in the car. We walked away so he couldn't hear the conversation.

"Can I take you away for the night?" he said softly. "Dinner and a movie to relax and unwind?"

"Dinner and a movie for sure." I smiled. "The relax and unwind ... not too sure about that. What exactly do you mean by *relax and unwind*?"

"You joining me for a night of conversation and laughter."

"Time will tell," I said, smelling the roses. "I'll have to see how dinner goes first. So far, you have been a man of your word. I think I might just be able to trust you."

"Oh, yes, Pretty, you can trust me. I want to make your graduation night special."

I hugged him and said, "Meet me at this same place tonight at eight."

Flashing that million-dollar smile, he said, "Will do, beautiful."

I turned and walked back to the car where my dad sat waiting and looking like he was about to explode. I got in the car and closed the door, and my dad said, "Baby, he's not to be trusted. He has a deep secret within."

I sighed. "Oh, stop it, Daddy. Every man I meet you are against. You see fault in every man."

"Pretty, he's bad news, and I don't want you ever seeing him again. Please give him the roses and gift back, sweetie. This man is bad news."

"Dad, N. works two jobs. He's not a drug dealer or anything like that, okay? I made sure of that."

He placed his hand on my shoulder and said, "Please listen to me this time, if you never listen to me again. He has a secret, baby. This is not the guy for you."

I looked at him and said, "Daddy, I'm eighteen, and I'm grown. I can pick a man on my own. You are wrong about him; he is a good person. I think I may have found the man of my dreams."

As he took his hand off my shoulder, he said it again. "Please leave him alone."

I told him, "Can't do that, Dad. Just know you raised a good girl. I know bad news when I see it."

Daddy looked away, and I pulled out my cell and called down to Texturz Hair Salon to reach my stylist, Mrs. Keisha, to see if I could come in really quickly just to get my hair flat ironed again. It was done already, but I wanted it to look like it was fresh and new. Of course, she said, "Sure." I told her that I had to drop off my dad and I would be there.

I ran inside the house when I dropped off Daddy to show my mom my gifts and to put the roses in a vase. Out of the blue, my mom said, "Your body is a temple. Treat it with respect … save it for your husband. One night can change your life."

Running out the house to go get my hair flat ironed, I looked at her and said, "Okay, Mom, I know."

When I got to the salon, I told Mrs. Keisha all about my day. She said, "Baby, be careful. Everything that looks good isn't always good for you."

I then decided to stop talking about N. Nobody wanted to hear my good news. I'd finally found the right one. One day had made a difference in my life. I sat in that chair while getting my hair done thinking about what my parents said to me about N., but they were wrong. He was a good man. They just didn't want me to date anyone.

"All done," Mrs. Keisha said. "Be safe and remember … one night can change your life."

I said, "Okay, thanks," and I paid her and walked out the door. I called N. and told him thanks again and that I looked forward to meeting him for dinner and whatever the night brought. Look at me, I must have lost my mind for a minute. I wasn't supposed to say anything like that. That would make him think that I was open for anything. Well, I guess you can say that, at that time, I was. I was feeling that this fly guy had bought me something that no man had ever bought me before—dozens of roses—and he talked with a good conversation. He had two jobs and was from Florida. No one in the Mil-town had ever had him before. He was a keeper.

I rushed home to take a shower and put on the fly dress that N. had bought me. I almost fell out looking at myself in the mirror. I was so fine, and it fit me perfectly. I thought, "Wow, he has great taste." I pulled out my Mac makeup and went to work. I didn't need a lot; I'm a natural beauty. I just wanted to enhance my eyes and lips a little. After that, I called my homegirls and told them about the outfit and roses and that I was on my way to meet N. That's when Kim said, "Pretty, are you sure his name isn't Tony?"

I said, "Girl, yes! I got to go."

All of a sudden, Kim sounded like something was wrong. "Wait, my cousin Nia wants to talk to you … you know—the one that is saved and loves the Lord?"

I said, "Okay. Please hurry."

Nia got on the phone and said, "Hi, Pretty. You have been on my heart today. I just want to tell you that God loves you, and he is ready for you to serve him completely. Going to church isn't enough. Get in your word. He makes it plain and simple how we must live to please him. I'm not sure where you're on your way to, but I feel led to tell you not to go—don't do it. It's a trap from the Enemy. There is this motivational speaker named LaTonia who has a site that will uplift, encourage, and motivate you to become the woman of God that God created you to be. Before you leave the house, please go to her site. It's called http://www.sistersbuildingsisters.com; I know it will bless you."

I said, "Thanks, and bye. I'm running late, and I have to go."

She said, "Please visit the site before you go."

I said, "Okay, put Kim back on." We said a small prayer, and I was on my way.

I grabbed my overnight bag just in case I decided to stay all night with N. at the hotel. As I reached for the doorknob to leave my bedroom and head out, I became very lightheaded. It was like I wasn't seeing clearly. I reached for the doorknob again, and it seemed like it was getting worse, but I was determined to go on this date.

After all, he was a fly guy, a man of his word from a different state, and a virgin. He was a keeper for real. I ran past my parents; I didn't want to hear them say all of the things they had been saying to me and my sister forever. I said, "Be back. Love you all, and don't wait up for me."

Once I got in the car and put my seat belt on and turned the ignition, the car didn't say one word. Now, come on, this was a brand-new 2009 Lexus. I had never had a problem with my car before. I tried it at least three times, and nothing happened—not one sound came from the car. It was as if there was no life in it—a 2009, brand-new Lexus. I thought, "What is really going on?" I tried one last time, and it started as if nothing was ever wrong with it from the start.

Okay, my mind was playing tricks on me. I knew that I had been listening to Keyshia Cole when I'd gotten out of the car the last time, but somehow "I Need You Now" by Smokie Norful was playing. I thought, "What in the world is going on? All I need right now is to reach N., the man of my dreams. Later for all of the Jesus stuff. I love you, Lord, but I'm on my way to see another great man."

I thought, "After the long talk from Kim's cousin Nia, almost about to pass out trying to reach for the doorknob, and my brand-new Lexus not starting up right away, this better be a night that I will never forget."

I finally made it. While parking, I look in my rearview mirror, and who did I see? Nehemiah … looking like a million dollars, plus some, with a few females approaching him. I know ole boy ain't crazy. One thing I don't tolerate is disrespect; but this guy is fine, fly, well groomed, and dressed from head to toe. Who wouldn't want him?

I reached in my purse to call my homegirls to let them know that I was there and that I would call them from time to time to share how the night was going. "Okay, girls, got to go—here comes N. Look at this! He has another dozen of roses in his hands! He's too much … but not too much for *me*."

I opened the car door, and he said, "No, Pretty, that's my job."

I looked at him and smiled. "Boy, please. Be who you are and stop trying to be the perfect gentleman."

He laughed as he closed my door.

"You look very beautiful tonight."

"Thank you."

We looked in each other's eyes for a quick second, and then my cell phone rang. I had to answer it.

"Hi, Mom."

She said, "Pretty, the Enemy comes in more ways than one."

While talking to my mom, I heard N.'s cell phone ring. He answered and said, "Tony speaking." I looked; I could have sworn he'd said *Tony*. I said, "Mom, okay, and I know all that already. Trust me; I'm not with the Enemy." Little did I know that one night was about to change my life.

I hung my mom up and said, "Excuse me, N. Did I hear you say 'Tony speaking?'"

He said, "What, baby? I said, 'Talk to me.'"

I said, "Oh, I must be tripping." Then I said, "Okay, what's next?"

He said, "Keep your car parked here. I have a surprise for you."

I said, "Oh, no, Mister. I don't think so."

"Trust me. I haven't lied to you yet. You're in good hands, I promise you. I arranged for a nice dinner in the hotel room. And I have candles and flowers waiting for you, Ms. Pretty." All the while, he was flashing that million-dollar smile.

"Boy, look, I told you once before, you got the wrong one, baby. I don't sleep around. I'm a virgin, and I'm going to keep it that way until I'm married."

He said, "Girl, you must have been through some things before. I don't want to sleep with you. I'm a virgin also. I just want to be somewhere where there is no one but you and me getting to know one another."

My mind was saying, "No, girl, don't go." But this dude was so fly and had been real so far. I thought, "Why not? Oh, yeah … his plates say that."

I said, "Excuse me, N. I need to make a personal call real quick."

"Go right ahead, Pretty," he said, watching me as I walked away.

I called my homegirl Mia. I said, "Mia, I'm going to leave my car here at the strip mall while I jump in the car with N. and go have dinner. Remember, girl, his plates say, "'Why not.'"

She laughed and said, "Be safe, Pretty. I love you. Be safe."

While walking back over to where he was standing, I saw this black Nissan pull up, and someone yelled out, "T baby!" Well, I'd *thought* she'd said, "T baby," but that wouldn't make any sense. His name starts with an *N*, not *T*. I thought, "Boy, oh boy, I'm hungry and hearing things. I need to eat."

So I said, "N., let's do this. Ms. Pretty is hungry."

He laughed and opened my door. I looked and said, "Boy, I told you once," and smiled.

"Girl, just get in and relax," he said as he reached over and buckled my seat belt.

Lord have mercy, it was clean as a whistle inside that dude's car, and it smelled good just like him. Lord, please help me. I sat there thinking about the song by Smokie Norful, "I Need You Now." Help me, Lord; I'm having impure thoughts about this man. I don't want my thoughts to become actions. Because Lord knows that's how things get started. We think, and then we act on our thoughts.

"Nehemiah, where are we going?"

"Relax, Pretty. Didn't I say you can trust me?"

"Look," I said. "Learn how to answer questions with answers and stop getting slick at the mouth."

He said, "I bet you got spankings all the time when you were a child."

I said, "Why would you say that?"

He said, "Your mouth."

We both laughed, and I told him, "It's not like Burger King; you can't have it your way. My saying is 'It's either my way or no way.' I'm spoiled, and I get what I want."

He said, "Okay, then, tonight's your night. You can have it your way."

I smiled, he smiled, and I turned my head to look out the window. "Wow! These are some nice homes out here. N., where you taking me?"

He said, "Girl, you ask too many questions."

We slowly pulled into a nice area in Mequon, and on the top of a building, I saw a sign that said Relax and Unwind Here at the Sybaris. N. parked the car and told me, "I will be right back. Let me check out a few things."

I said, "Okay."

When he stepped out, I hurried up and called Maya and said, "Girl, we at this place called the Sybaris in Mequon. Yes ... here he comes—got to go." He came to my side of the car and opened up the door. Then told me to go in the place. I thought, "Lord, please don't let this dude be a killer."

I said, "You go first."

He said, "Go 'head, you can trust me."

I pushed the room door in really quickly and stepped back. N. was laughing so hard. He said, "It's all good, Pretty." I then pushed it open further ... and oh, my goodness ... roses everywhere, petals all on the floor, candles lit ... and he was playing the song "Customer" by Raheem DeVaughn. I turned to look in the other direction, and there was a bed, Jacuzzi, and a swimming pool. I thought, "I must be dreaming!"

I said, "So, player, how do you know about something so classy like this?"

He said, "I asked my homeboys Dante and Boo, and they told me a young lady such as yourself would love this. They come here quite often to get away from the madness."

"Well, Dante and Boo must got it going on if this is a place they come to often. This is something you see on TV. Nehemiah, you sure you haven't brought none of your girlfriends here before? Mr. N., how many kids you got?"

"I told you, Pretty, I'm a virgin. I have no children."

"Okay, dude. Look, you fine, fly, got two jobs, a nice ride, and you're the perfect gentleman. You have no woman or kids. You must be gay."

He laughed.

I said, "I'm serious."

He said, "No, Pretty. My grandmother raised me well and taught me how to treat a woman."

I said, "Oh, okay, I see now. Grandma raised you, so that's where the perfect gentleman came from. Why didn't your parents raise you?"

He paused. "My parents died shortly after I was born. So my grandmother raised me."

I wanted to ask him how they died. But I could tell that he was getting a little emotional, so I didn't say one word. I changed the subject. "What's for dinner? I'm starving. Plus I don't want to be out too late. I need my beauty sleep."

He laughed as he took the lids off the trays.

"Oh, my, soul food ... greens, dressing, yams, and baked chicken. Who cooked all this?"

"Mrs. Syn and her daughters Ebony, Jasmine, and Monique. They have a catering business. She cooks like my granny cooks—from the heart. Yeah, she's my homeboy Dante's mom. Her food is so good, Pretty."

"I bet. Let me go wash my hands so I can taste Mrs. Syn's cooking. I may need her to cater a party or something for me one day."

I went to wash my hands, and when I came back, there were two gift bags—one big one and one small one. I said, "Thank you. I'll open them after we eat dinner." I felt so special. So far, this was the perfect night. N. said the prayer before we ate, and after he finished, it was on.

"N., you wasn't lying. This food is good! Make sure to give me Mrs. Syn's number."

He smiled with his million-dollar smile and said, "I told you that you would love it."

We laughed and talked while eating. After I was done, I walked over to him and kissed him on his cheek. He said, "Thanks, Pretty."

I said, "No, thank you. You really know how to treat a young lady. Now for the gifts."

He wanted me to open the big one first. I reached inside the bag and saw a tag that said Designs by Tuesdai. I pulled out a pair of jeans and a shirt that fitted me just right. I screamed and said, "Thank you, N.! Thank you!"

He said, "Tuesdai's a one-of-a-kind denim designer."

I said, "I see. Ole girl is cold with the rhinestones. Okay, let me open the other gift. Oh, my goodness, this is a swimwear set." The swimsuit was gorgeous, and it had matching flip-flops and a swim robe. This dude was too much … but not too much for me. Just my type.

He said, "Go try them all on."

I said, "Okay—be right out." I put on the jean set, and boy oh boy, did I look like a million dollars. Ms. Tuesdai knows her stuff, and he was right on point.

I stepped out, and his eyes got so big. He said, "Dang, you fine. You look so pretty, Pretty."

I said, "Thanks to you for the outfit—and my parents for my looks."

I then tried on the swimwear. I thought, "Lord, Jesus, I'm so fine." I knew that once I stepped out, he was going to fall out. I walked out, and his mouth dropped.

He was speechless.

I laughed. "Say something."

He said, "You look like a queen, baby. Go 'head, girl, and wear that swimsuit."

I walked over to him and gave him a hug. "Your turn. Where are your trunks so we can test the pool together?"

He said, "Be right back," and he went to change. Wow! He stepped out, and I almost fell out. This dude was breathtaking—too fine to describe. We looked in each other's eyes, and all I could see was lust. We both got in the water and played for awhile. After about an hour, I was tired and wanted some sleep.

We got out of the pool, and I took a hot shower to get the chlorine off my body. While showering, I thought, "Should I stay, or should I go?" And of course, something was saying, "Go," but I wanted to stay. So I did, and one thing led to another. Little did I know that one night was about to change my life. I came a virgin … and was leaving a fornicator. Was it worth it? Yes, indeed. I got a good man and a few other things. I had no regrets.

The next day, I awoke to N. on the phone saying, "I will be there."

I thought, "Be *where*?" I thought, "Don't get hurt. And who is he talking to?" My mom always told me that my body is a temple, and once you give it up, everything changes—including your attitude and emotions.

I looked at him and said, "Who is that?"

He said, "My aunt. My grandmother is ill, and I have to get back to Florida."

I said, "What? You got to *leave*?"

He said, "Pretty, yes, baby. I have to go see about my grandmother."

I said, "Whatever." I got up and got in the shower and started to cry. I'd just had sex with a man I didn't really know, and I liked him like crazy, and now he had to go.

He came in the bathroom while I was in the shower and said, "Look, Pretty. You are done with school. I will send for you once I get there, and you can come and meet my family. Don't think this one night is the end."

I said, "Okay. You have been a man of your word this far. I trust you, baby. Give me a second; I'm almost done."

He said, "Okay, let me go take care of the bill."

I said, "Okay, and thanks for last night. I will never forget it."

"I bet you won't," he said, and he laughed and walked out the door.

In the shower, I felt awful. I thought, "What have I done to myself? I have always vowed to save myself for marriage. Oh, well—this won't be the last bad choice I make in life. At least I was his first, and he was mine, and it was worth it. I got gifts and was treated like the queen I am."

While I was drying off, he walked in with a strange look on his face and said, "You ain't done yet? Let's roll out."

I said, "Excuse me? Give me a second."

He said, "I don't have a second."

I said, "Okay, I know your grandma needs you, but don't come to me like that."

"Tramp, please."

I looked and said, "What did you say?"

He said, "Let's go."

I thought, "Now I know I ain't crazy. Homeboy just called me a tramp. Okay, okay, maybe I'm tripping now. I'll let that ride …"

I said, "One second, baby."

He replied, "My name is Nehemiah, not 'baby.'"

I said, "Oh, okay … Nehemiah."

See, I was excusing his behavior because he was in his feelings about his grandmother. I thought, "I know he don't mean to come off this way toward me, Ms. Pretty. He was at me too hard to be treating me like this. Plus, I'm a dime piece, and it's a blessing for him to have me."

I said, "N., I'm going to be praying for you and your family."

He said, "We good. Be praying for yourself."

I walked out the door and headed to the car. Keep in mind that I had the two gift bags and my overnight bag in my hands. I was expecting him to at least open the door. After all, that's what he had been waiting to do for me all yesterday. Instead, he pushed his alarm button and opened his door and looked at me as if to say, "Hurry up."

Okay, now, this is it. Nehemiah is about to get told a thing or two. I put the bags in the back, slammed the door, and got in the front. I looked at N., and he wasn't showing that million-dollar smile anymore. And he wasn't looking as fine as he had the day before. His whole demeanor had changed. All I could hear was my mom saying, "Your body is a temple, and once you give it up, things change—attitudes and emotions."

I reached over to touch his hand, and his cell phone rang. He picked it up and said, "T speaking." I was shocked. I knew that I'd heard him say *T.* The smile appeared again, and his conversation changed. I was getting upset, because he sounded like he did when he was talking to me when we first met, which was just yesterday. I looked at him as if to say, "What's up?"

And he looked at me as if to say, "Can I help you?"

I thought, "Okay, now, I must be dreaming. I have given this man my body and mind plus time, and he acting like this." My eyes watered up. My heart raced; I was ready to bust him in his head. I thought, "Okay, let me calm down and control my feelings. Wow! Mommy told me it would be like this."

Twenty minutes later, we were almost back where I'd left my car, and he was still on the phone. I was just listening to his conversation, and it had to be a female he was talking to like that.

We finally reached my car, and he put the phone down and said, "Pretty, I will get with you later."

I said, "No hug or kiss? No making sure I get in the car?"

He said, "I'll call you."

I got out, and he pulled off. Tears rolled down my face. There was no way this could be happening to me, Ms. Pretty. As I opened my car door, all kinds of thoughts crossed my mind, so I reached inside my purse and grabbed my cell to call him. His voicemail came on. It said, "What's up? Leave me a message, and I will make sure to hit you back." I was shocked. Remember yesterday when it was personal for me? So I tried again, and he answered.

"Hey, N., what's up?"

"I'm on the other line with a good friend. I'll call you once I hit the highway."

I said, "Will I see you before you leave?"

He said, "Probably not. I need to get my hair cut and make a few runs before I go. I'll call you later."

He hung up. I was in shock. My heart dropped, and tears flowed. I got in my car and just sat for about an hour crying and asking myself, "What have I done to myself?"

Then my cell rang. I rushed to answer it, thinking that it was him, but it was my homegirls, so I had to pull myself together. I answered, and they said, "Where are you? And who does N. have in his car? He just drove past us." I felt sick to my stomach.

I said, "Oh, was it his homeboy or homegirl?"

They said, "His homegirl."

I played it off and said, "That's his cousin."

They said, "Oh, she looked a little like you."

"I know. I met her last night," I lied. I couldn't let them know that I didn't know who she was. I said, "Girls, I'm on my way home. Let me call and tell you all about the night once I make it there."

They said, "Okay, Pretty, hurry up! We can't wait."

I hung up the phone and cried, cried, cried. While driving, I called N. again. He answered, and I heard a female in the background. I said, "Who's that?"

He said, "A pretty young lady I met a while back," as if that was okay to say to me.

I said, "What?"

He said, "Pretty, don't call me. I will call you," and he hung up.

I called right back, and I got his voicemail.

Can you imagine how I felt? Oh, Lord, it hurt my head and my heart. I looked in my mirror, and I looked a mess. I thought, "I can't go home like this. My parents will know that I've been crying. And what would I say? 'I lost my virginity to a fine guy I knew for only one day from Florida, with a million-dollar smile and a slick ride, and now he's treating me like trash'? I don't think so."

My dad had already told me that N. was bad news. And my mom told me to save myself for marriage. I thought, "I guess I will go sit in the Shorewood High School parking lot for a while to pray and think and fix my face."

Wow! It seemed like one night changed my life. I used to be a virgin with a strong belief in waiting until I was married. I had self-respect, class, and a positive attitude with goals and dreams. Now I felt like nothing … lost, confused, and downright dirty. I opened my life and gave my body to a man I barely knew because he was fine, fly, had a nice ride, and he gave me a few gifts. I thought, "Maybe he will call me soon and say that he was just playing to see how I would react. After all, I'm pretty, and he was blessed to have me."

While I was sitting in the parking lot, I saw a truck pull up, and it was a few ladies bringing in tables and chairs. They were always having something at the high school. I wondered what was going on.

I got out after I fixed my face, and I asked one of the ladies, "What's going on here?"

She said, "Hi, my name is Mrs. Syn. I cater for all kinds of events, all kinds of food. They're having a banquet tonight for the teachers."

I said, "Oh, okay."

As I walked away, it dawned on me that she had to be the lady that catered our food. I went back up to her and said, "Are you Dante's mother, and do you have three daughters?"

She said, "Yes, how do you know Dante?"

I said, "I don't—a friend of mine does … the guy Nehemiah that you catered the food for last night."

She said, "I'm sorry, that name doesn't ring a bell. I'm so busy on the move, I forget a few." She laughed. I asked her for a card and told her how good the food was. She gave me a card and asked me if I was I okay. She said that it looked like I had been crying. I told her that I was good and that it was nice to meet her, and then I walked away.

I thought, "Wow! If she can tell, I know my parents will be able to tell that something is wrong with me. Lord, what have I done to myself? I feel a mess. All this time, I vowed to keep my body for my husband. And now I've given it to a total stranger just because he bought me a few gifts and made me feel special. Please forgive me, God."

Once I got inside my car, I put my seat belt on and turned on the radio. The song that was playing was "Customer." Tears poured down my face. I reached inside my bag to see if I had missed his call. There was only one missed call … from my dad's cell phone.

Wow! It hurt so badly that it took my breath away. I said to myself, "Okay, Pretty, get it together," and I looked in the mirror. I put my Mac lip gloss on and drove to my house—crying and talking to myself all the way there, asking myself, "Why?"

Before I pulled up to the house, I decided to give N. another call. I dialed his number and hung up. I was afraid of what he might say, and I didn't want to cry anymore.

So I decided to wait until later to call. I drove up, and my dad and sister were outside washing my mom's car.

My dad said to me, "Pretty, where have you been? We were worried sick about you."

I said, "Dad, remember I told you and Mom not to wait up for me because I was going to be out all night? I hung out with a few of my homegirls and spent the night with them."

He trusted me, because I had always been honest with my parents. I thought, "Wow! Look at me—I lost my virginity, and now I'm lying to my dad." After talking to Daddy, I was walking up the stairs to go inside the house, and he said, "Pretty, you know the boy you introduced me to yesterday?"

"Yes, Daddy."

"Your mom and I seen him at the mall earlier with a young lady. I thought it was you for a minute, until she turned around. I tell you, he's bad news. I have the gift of discernment. He's up to no good. Good thing you obeyed me and didn't deal with him."

I said, "Okay, Daddy." I almost busted out crying right then and there.

I held back the tears as I walked in the house. As soon as I came in, my mom said, "Pretty, I had this bad feeling last night every time I thought about you. I'm so glad you are okay."

"I'm fine, Mom," I said, running up to my room. I needed to pray right away.

"Okay, Lord, I know I pray every other day, but today I'm down on my knees. Lord, please forgive me. I have shamed you and my family. Lord, I'm angry and ready to commit a crime. I need you now, Lord, I need you now.

I'm hurting inside, Lord. I feel so nasty and disgusted with myself. How did I allow this to happen to me? Lord, please take this pain away. I trust that you will, Lord, in Jesus's name. Amen."

I got up and washed my face, and my cell phone rang. I almost broke my neck trying to answer it.

"Hello?"

"Hi, Pretty."

"Hey, N. ..." I said with a smile on my face so wide.

He said, "What's up?"

I said, "I thought you forgot about me."

He laughed. "Forget about you? How could I do that, you slut?"

I said, "What?"

He said, "You were easy. You were just the type I wanted to bless."

I said, "*Bless?*"

He said, "Yeah, tramp. I left you with a beautiful blessing. You will *never* forget about me."

"Trust me; I won't be having no baby," I said, wishing I'd taken his number out my cell from the start.

"Sure won't. Your blessing won't get eighteen years old and leave you. The blessing I gave you will last as long as you live."

He laughed and hung up on me.

I thought, "I must be having a nightmare. Did he just call me a slut and a tramp? And he thinks he got me pregnant. Okay, okay, let me calm down. I'm on fire now. Lord, please, please help me. Okay, I got to get out of here. I'm about to go crazy." I grabbed my purse and car keys and ran out of the house.

My mom screamed, "Pretty, what's going on?"

I yelled back with a lie. "I'm good, Mom. I'm running late for a job interview."

I don't like lying to my parents. But I had to get out of there. I would have gone crazy at home. I needed to talk to one of my homegirls. I couldn't handle this all by myself. I grabbed my phone and called Kim.

My voice was shaking. I said, "Kim, I need you, girl."

She said, "What's wrong? And where are you?"

I told her, "Come out. I'm almost in front of your house."

She ran out as I pulled up. She jumped in, and I pulled off.

Before I could get anything out, Kim said, "Pretty, pull over now and get out." She hugged me and said, "Calm down and get yourself together. Get in the car and let me drive."

Now, my girl Kim didn't play, so she wasn't going to be too happy to hear what I had to say. She drove in front of Oakland Gyros and parked. She looked at me and said, "Spit it out now."

I told the story as tears fell from my eyes—how I slept with him and how he had been treating me badly since that morning, calling me tramp, slut, trash, and a few other names. Oh, Lord, I still remember the look of disappointment on Kim's face.

She said, "What? You did what? Pretty, you vowed to God and yourself to save yourself for marriage. Why, girl? Why?"

"Kim, it was just something about *him* that made me do it."

"What? Because he was fine, fly, and from Florida? Are you kidding me? Did you use protection?"

"No, why would I? He was a virgin, just like me."

She looked as if she'd seen a ghost and said, "You have lost your mind, girl. I know you're joking about using no protection."

I said, "No, Kim. He looked … healthy, and he was a virgin."

She got out the car and said, "Lord, help me right now before I choke my friend to death."

I got out the car and said, "Kim, help me, please. I'm hurting. I can't stay home tonight. My parents will be able to tell that something is wrong."

She said, "Give me his number—now." I gave her the number, and she called him and said, "Hello, Nehemiah?"

N. said, "No, I'm sorry. You got the wrong number."

He hung up on her, and she said, "Pretty, what did you say his number was?"

I showed Kim the number I had in my cell phone, and she said, "That's what I dialed. Let me do this again." She dialed it for the second time, thinking that she had dialed too quickly before and had probably dialed it incorrectly.

Again, N. answered the phone. But this time, before Kim could say anything, he said, "Listen, there is no Nehemiah that has this number. Never was. This phone belongs to me—Tony."

When Kim heard the name Tony, she dropped the phone and said, "Pretty, what have you done?"

I picked the phone up and said, "Nehemiah, why are you doing this?"

He said, "Girl, my name ain't Nehemiah; it's Tony. You fell for the okie-doke, and I won. I finished my mission. Now I can go back to Florida and enjoy the rest of my days."

I screamed and called him every name I could think of, Lord, help me. One night changed my life. I hung up the phone, and Kim looked at me and said, "Pretty, this isn't good."

I said, "What are you talking about, Kim?"

"Remember when I kept asking you if his name was Tony?"

"Yes, what about it?"

"I asked you that because my homeboys, Boo and Dante, said that they heard that this dude named Tony was using a fake name and was on a mission to 'bless' any woman that would allow him to."

I remembered that N. had called Boo and Dante his homeboys when we were at the Sybaris, so I raised an eyebrow. "You know Boo and Dante?"

"Yeah, they real cool," she said, nodding her head. "Two young men about they business. They warned me to be on the watch because ole dude seemed shady—like he had something up his sleeve. He would always ask them if they knew a spot to take classy young ladies, because he had a gift he wanted to give them. And he wanted to give them the gift at a place that they would never forget. They told him about the Sybaris because they thought he was a cool dude, until Boo—he's the one that thinks a lot—said ole boy on something dirty." Kim paused for a second and said, "Pretty, baby, I'm afraid one night has changed your life."

I took a deep breath and said, "Kim, would you please call your homeboys Boo and Dante?"

She called them and let me speak to them. I said, "Hi. Do you both know a dude by the name of Nehemiah from Florida?"

They said, "Yep, we met this dude 'Nehemiah' that said he was from Florida, but his name is Tony. If you cross his path, don't deal with him. He's up to no good. We would hate to see any woman done wrong and mistreated."

I gave Kim back the phone, and I cried like a baby as I sat back in the car. As she hung up the phone, I heard Kim saying, "He's going to reap what he sow." Then she said, "Pretty, what's your mom's cell phone number? I'm going to ask if you can stay the night at my house. And first thing in the morning, you're going to the clinic to get tested for everything."

I gave her my mom's number. She called, and Mom told her that my staying overnight would be fine. Kim gathered all of our homegirls up, and we all stayed the night at her house. She told the story as I rested in her bed and cried, and they felt my pain. See, my friends and I really love one another. We are like sisters for real. We always have one another's back.

Kim said, "Do you know any way to contact Tony's mom?"

I said, "No, his parents are deceased, and he lives in Florida with his grandmother. Well, at least that's the lie he told."

"Well, has he ever said his grandma's name?"

I shook my head, and I told her, "But the gift bag that I have came from his sister's boutique, and it has a phone number on it."

She said, "I will be calling after we leave the clinic tomorrow."

I thought, "Wow! Yesterday, I graduated from high school—just as happy and feeling on top of the world. Today, I feel like crap with no direction. I can't believe one night changed my life."

I told my homegirls, "Okay, girls, let's pray. I'm tired and need some sleep."

Kim's cousin said, "Did you go to that website I told you about?"

I said, "No, girl—my fault. I was rushing to get to N. I mean, Tony ... or whatever his name is. I wish I would have. Maybe I wouldn't be here looking a mess and feeling so bad about myself. My stylist, Mrs. Keisha, said, 'Everything that looks good ain't good for you.'"

They all nodded their heads in agreement, and we prayed. After we finished, Kim brought me some hot tea, and I fell straight to sleep. I slept for about four hours and got up to get some water and felt led to go on the site Nia was talking about. My friends were all asleep, and Kim's computer was in her room, so I didn't have to disturb anyone. I clicked on the site, and boy oh boy, what a blessing it was. I got to this one topic called "The Stop Sign," and the founder of the site was talking about warning signs and how God sends them to warn us before destruction.

I thought about how dizzy I'd gotten when I was about to leave to meet him and how my dad knew that N. was bad news from just meeting him once ... and to top it all off, my brand-new car would not start up. Wow! I should have listened to Nia. She told me not to do whatever it was I was planning on doing last night. It's true; God sure will send someone to minister to you or to plant a seed in your life.

I thought, "Okay, let me click off from here. I'm crying all over again. This site called http://www.sistersbuildingsisters.com is a very inspirational site … it makes you think. Let me get some rest. I have a long day ahead of me. Tomorrow, I will be sitting at a clinic getting tested for every STD there is. No need to worry—he was a virgin, just like me."

Chapter 2

I awoke to all of my girls standing over me laughing with belts in their hands, saying, "Get up so we can spank your butt because you knew better."

We all laughed, and I said, "I deserve this spanking. I knew better. I fell right into the hands of the Enemy." Bishop Burt always preached about how the Enemy will make things look good that are deadly to you. Lord, I should have known better. I was too busy caught up in the bling and the dollars.

I picked up my towel and said, "Okay, girls, give me thirty minutes, and I will be ready to head out to the clinic." While I was in the shower, I hear Kim's cousin praying, "Father God, give Pretty the strength to endure whatever may be getting ready to surface or take place. Lord, forgive her and put your loving arms around her."

After I was done with showering and getting dressed, I walked out and said, "Nia, thanks for praying, girl," and gave her a hug. I looked at my homegirls and said, "Okay, girls, let's do this. Kim, you drive. I need to relax, because I'm a little nervous now. I don't know why, but I am."

"Okay. Which clinic, Pretty?" Kim asked.

I said, "I don't know. We never had to go to one. What about my doctor's office? I got the card."

Kim said, "Okay, call and see if your doctor can get you in on such short notice."

"Oh, wait," I said, wringing my hands. "Won't they tell my parents?"

Kim said, "No, you are grown, and that's personal."

"Okay, let me call."

I called, and they said, "Sure, come in. We had a cancellation."

So we headed down to my doctor's office. While driving, we passed the McDonald's on Capitol where I met N., or Tony, or whatever his name was. I wished I wouldn't have ever met him and fell for the trick of the Enemy. My parents always said, "If it doesn't line up with the word of God, it is no good for you."

Kim started blasting the music. As we got closer, my stomach bubbled, and I felt a little nervous. I don't know why. I thought, "I'm all good. He was a virgin, and so was I." The song "Touch My Body" came on, and my homegirls were singing it. I looked back and shouted, "Shut up!" They all looked at me like I was crazy. They all screamed back and said, "Next time, make better choices," and continued to sing. That was the last song I wanted to hear. I never wanted anyone else to touch my body. It caused too much emotional pain.

As we pulled up to the clinic, I said, "Okay, girls, here we are."

I couldn't believe that I was on my way into the doctor's office to have every STD test done. Two days ago, I was a high school graduate with big dreams and goals for my life. Today, I was having a test done for AIDS, herpes, gonorrhea, and chlamydia, and all the rest of the things that one can get when having unprotected sex and sex before marriage. Lord, have mercy. I thought, "I know I'm all good. N, I mean Tony, was well groomed and very clean … and a virgin. So, I know I'm all good."

We arrived at my doctor's office. I signed in, and the medical assistant called me back and said, "What seems to be the problem that brought you in today?"

As I started to tell her, the tears dropped from my eyes. Me, Ms. Pretty, had slipped up in a major way, and there was no turning back now. In a calm and sweet voice, the young woman said, "Baby, God is a forgiving God. All you have to do is confess to him and repent with a sincere heart and turn from those wicked ways and give your life to him. Everything will be all right. But, baby, remember—just because God forgives us, it doesn't mean that there won't be consequences for our actions."

I said, "Yes, ma'am." I then asked her what her name was, because I couldn't see her tag. She replied, "Jasmine."

I said to her, "Thank you so much, Ms. Jasmine, for those words of encouragement. I feel a little better now."

She smiled and then said to me, "Okay, Pretty, all of your lab work is done. I'll give you a minute to undress from the waist down, and then the doctor will be in for your first pap smear."

I was ready to get up and run out of there. My mom always said that she hated to have that done, so I didn't know what to expect—just like I didn't know what to expect when I laid down with N., I mean Tony. I thought, "Oh, Lord, what have I done to myself?"

So of course it took forever for the doctor to come in. That meant that I had more time to think. I grabbed my purse and called ole boy. He answered. I said, "Are you ready to talk now?"

He said, "There's nothing to talk about."

"Oh, no? Well, I want to know what your real name is. And why would you do me like this?"

He laughed. "It's Tony, and you did yourself this way. It was free choice, baby, and you chose me."

I said to him, "I chose you because I trusted you and thought you were a good man."

He said, "How could you trust someone you didn't know? You said you went to church. Didn't God say put your trust in no man? Well, I was that man you shouldn't have trusted. I'll holla," and he hung up.

Knock, knock … and the doctor came in.

My eyes were full of tears, and my heart was ready to explode from all of the pain that I'd brought on myself. I had been going to this doctor since I was a baby, and I was sitting there crying like I'd just lost one of my friends or family members.

She said, "Do you need a few minutes? Or can I get started with the exam?"

I said, "Let's get this done and over."

We started to talk, and I told her about everything that had taken place. I could tell that she was shocked, but she left her personal feelings out of it and stayed professional. The only thing she said was, "Pretty, if this ever takes place again, please, please make sure you use protection. All right?"

I nodded my head to let her know that I was listening, not that I planned on letting it ever happen again.

She then told me, "If any of the test results come back positive, we'll give you a call."

Oh, Lord, all kinds of thoughts crossed my mind …

Before she walked out the door, I said, "Thank you, Doctor. Please don't tell my parents that I was here."

She smiled. "No problem. I couldn't even if I wanted to."

I told myself, "Okay, Pretty, get yourself together. No need to worry. God's got it."

I walked out into the waiting room, and my friends looked at me like they were in shock. I said, "What's wrong?"

They whispered, "Your mom is here with your little sister for a checkup for camp."

"Oh, Lord," I thought. "Think fast, Pretty."

Before I could say anything, my mom tapped me on my back and said, "Pretty, what are you doing here?"

I had to think of a lie fast.

I smiled. "Hi, Mom. I'm here taking a TB test for the job I applied for."

She said, "Okay, baby. See you at home."

I felt like the scum of the earth for sure. I'd lied to both of my parents—something that I never did—I'd had sex with a stranger, and to top it all off, I'd broken a promise that I'd made to God.

"Let's go, girls, I'm ready. The doctor said that they would call if any of the results were positive."

When we got in the elevator, I told my homegirls how much I loved and appreciated them for always being true and being such good friends. I know that I'm blessed to have each and every one of them in my life—so blessed that if I would have told them that I'd decided to stay the night with ole boy in the hotel, they would have said, "Absolutely not," and they would have come to get me. So much for keeping a secret. What's done in the dark will come to light eventually.

I thought maybe after years went by, before we got married or something, we would have shared what took place with us on our first date. Now look—there is no us. There never was. I was blinded by the smile, the gifts, conversations, and the way he carried himself. Silly me …

"Okay, ladies, what's on the agenda for the day?"

They all looked at me and said, "Sleep. Job searching tomorrow. So we all are resting and relaxing while looking in the paper for job opportunities."

Kim yawned. "Pretty, you drive back. You seem to be doing a little better now." I agreed with her.

While driving, I thought about what the medical assistant had said. "God forgives, and we should turn from our wicked ways." I would never, ever do anything like that again. I thought, "One night could have changed my life." But I knew that all of the tests would come back negative. After all, I'd prayed for forgiveness, and we both were virgins.

Chapter 3

"Well, ladies, here we are. I will be in shortly; I need to make a quick phone call."

Maya said, while getting out the car, "Pretty, let it go. Don't call him. It will only upset you again."

"I'll be fine. I have to do this for closure."

I thought, "Wow, one night and now I need closure. You would have thought that we were together for years. *Puhleeze*, it was only one night." I said, "Maya, I promise that I won't allow this to bring me down."

Walking away, she smiled and said, "Okay, *you promised*."

I called him. He answered, and these were his exact words: "Look, girl, don't call my phone anymore. I got what I wanted and left you with a blessing."

I said, "And what blessing is that?"

Tony laughed and said, "You'll see in time."

My head dropped, and the tears came. I thought about my dad saying, "He's bad news." I thought about my mom saying, "Your body is a temple, so save it for marriage, because once you give it up, everything changes." I also thought about what my homegirls and I promised one another. We promised to always stand for something so that we wouldn't fall for anything. And I guess I fell for anything, believing that Tony was such a gentleman and a man of his word. I realized that it was all a part of his plan and game. I was always told, "Pray and be watchful, for the Enemy comes to kill, steal, and destroy."

How I wish I would have done just that …

To make a long story short, we all found good jobs and were waiting to see if we'd gotten accepted at Hampton University. I got a job with Mrs. Syn's catering service, and come to find out, the medical assistant, Jasmine, was one of her oldest daughters. I was blessed, because being with them encouraged me to let go of what had taken place and to stay focused on what was to come in my life. I was really happy about the changes taking place in me … until I got the call.

I noticed every day that the same number would call around the same time. The caller never left a message, so I didn't think twice about it. On this particular day, I answered it, and it was the doctor's office.

"Hello, is this Ms. Pretty Jones?"

I said, "Yes, who is this?"

"This is the doctor's office calling. We need you to come in, and—if possible—bring a close relative or friend with you."

I said to the nurse, "Tell me what is wrong."

She said, "I'm sorry, Ms. Jones. I can't do that. You'll have to come in and see your physician."

I thought, "I have to go in and see the doctor." My heart raced, and I felt lightheaded. Every thought you can imagine was running in my head. I thought, "Okay, let me calm down and call my homegirls." I called all of them, and they were at work. The only person that was available was Kim's cousin Nia.

I said, "Nia, could you please go with me to the doctor? They want me to bring someone along."

She said, "Sure, come get me. I'm already ready."

I thought, "Oh, Lord, can I even drive?" I was scared out of my mind. I hadn't called N. … Tony … whatever his name was in a few weeks. I thought, "I got to call now to ask what he's done to me." I called the number, and the phone was no longer in service. I called again to make sure that I wasn't dialing the wrong number, and it said the same thing. "The number you have dialed is no longer in service." I took a deep breath and tried to stay calm. In a minute, I pulled up to Kim's house to get Nia, and off to the doctor we went.

Along the way, she said to me, "God is able, Pretty."

"Able to do what?" I said, hoping that she wouldn't start up. "I don't feel like hearing all that foolishness right now, Nia. Please, girl, give it a rest. I'm only going to talk about birth control or something like that." Little did I know that one night had changed my life.

We made it, and I could barely walk to the elevator—I was shaking and sweating so badly. I was so nervous! I made it to the front desk and told them who I was and that I had an appointment to speak with the doctor.

Nia looked at me and said again, "He's able, Pretty."

I thought, "Lord, why did I bring this girl with me? She's working my nerves!"

"Okay, Pretty. Please come with me," the nurse said. "Also, bring along your friend."

I thought, "Okay, now I need my parents. I'm so scared that I'm about to throw up. Lord, please help me. I got this feeling that it's bad news. Oh, Lord, please don't let me be pregnant. That's the worst thing it could be, because, N.—I mean Tony—was a virgin."

I reached the room, and the doctor was already sitting at the table. She could see that I was sweating and very uncomfortable. So she said, "Would you like some water?"

I told her, "I'm fine. Please go ahead and tell me why I'm here."

She looked at Nia and then back over at me. "Is it okay to discuss everything in front of your friend?"

I said, "Yes, please tell me."

She said, "Pretty, you are not pregnant."

I was so happy, and I calmed down after that. I thought, "I know for sure now that I'm here to talk about birth control."

She then said, "Do you remember the test we took a few weeks back?"

I said, "Yes."

She said, "All of the results came in a few days ago. We tried calling but could never get you on the phone. Pretty, I'm afraid I have some very bad news to tell you."

I said, "What? I got a yeast infection?"

She said, "No, sweetie. You tested positive for HIV."

I thought I was hearing things, so I said, "What? I didn't hear you."

The doctor repeated herself. I had tested positive for HIV.

I fell to my knees screaming as loudly as I could, saying, "Why, Lord? *Why me?*"

I thought, "Please, Lord, wake me up from this nightmare."

I remember them fanning me and putting a cold towel on my head. As they picked me up from off the floor, I said, "Okay, okay—wait a minute. I was a virgin, and he was a virgin. How did this happen? Retest me, Doctor; this is a mistake. Oh, God! Do I really have HIV?"

"Yes, Pretty. You have HIV," she said, handing me a box of tissue.

I screamed, "Oh, Lord, I can't take it! Please call my parents!" I told myself, "I'm dreaming … I'm dreaming." I screamed, "Someone, please help me! Please, please help me!"

Nia hugged and rocked me in her arms, saying, "Pretty, he's able."

The nurse went and called my parents. I screamed and cried on and on, asking the Lord to help me and to please take all of this pain away from me. What had I done to myself? I no longer want to live. I thought, "I'm going to find Tony and kill him. He lied! He wasn't a virgin!"

My cell phone rang, and Nia answered it. It was Kim, screaming at the top of her lungs and saying, "Where is Pretty? I have some bad news to give her!"

I heard Nia saying softly, "Listen, she can't handle any more bad news. We're at her doctor's office waiting for her parents to come."

Kim said, "Look, I need to tell her what we just found out through Dante and Boo about the guy she messed with from Florida."

Nia said, "Now is not the time."

I took the phone and said, "What, Kim? What?"

She said, "Pretty, he's dead."

I said, "What?"

"He's *dead*. Tony had a terrible accident on the highway going back to Florida. That's probably why you never heard from him again."

"Oh, God …" I dropped the phone and passed out.

When I woke up, I was in St. Mary's Hospital with IV fluids running through my veins and my arms tied down to the bed. I looked up. My parents and all of my homegirls were there. My mom and dad looked like they had been crying for days.

Daddy walked up to me and said, "Baby, why didn't you listen to me? I never told you anything wrong," and he fell down on my forehead, crying. My mom's face was so red, and her eyes were so puffy, I couldn't even look at her. I told Kim to pinch me because I must be dreaming.

She said, "Pretty, it's true, baby. It's all true. This is not a dream."

"What's true?" I had forgotten everything that had taken place. I was drugged up, I guess.

Kim asked my parents, "Is it okay if I tell Pretty what has happened?"

They said yes, and they stood by my bedside while she told me that I had HIV and that Tony had died in a car accident on his way back to Florida. I went crazy, screaming at the top of my lungs, saying, "Why? Why? Why did this happen to me? I'm going to kill him. He lied! He wasn't a virgin."

Although Kim had just told me that he was dead, I guess I refused to believe that. I was angry, upset, confused, disappointed, and I was so embarrassed. I'd let my parents, God, and my friends down. Most of all,

I'd let myself down. All my life, I'd had big dreams and goals. But I'd allowed a perfect stranger to come into my life and turn it upside down. Actually, I was to blame. I'd known better. I'd been warned. God used many signs to let me know not to do what I did. I played with Satan on his playground. Anything that doesn't line up with the word of God is no good for you. Wow! One night changed my life.

Time went on, and my family and I dealt with all of the things that came from having HIV. I had one thing left to do, and that was to contact Tony's sister in Florida to see if the other women he had slept with were aware of his having HIV. I had a card with her boutique name on it. I called and told her who I was; of course, she had no clue. I still didn't believe that Tony was dead, so I asked her if that was true. She told me that the car accident and his having HIV was all true.

I said, "I wish he hadn't lied to me about being a virgin when we first met."

His sister said, "Baby, from what I know, Tony *was* a virgin. He got HIV from our mom and his dad."

I repeated what his sister said out loud.

Tears began to fall from my eyes, and my mom took the phone and started talking with his sister. "So you're saying that your brother wasn't out here bad? That he got HIV from his parents?"

She replied, "Yes, ma'am. I'm so sorry that he used his anger and rage out on your daughter. He knew he had HIV ever since he was seven when my grandmother told him how our mom and his dad passed away. He left Florida upset and said that he was going on a mission. We never knew what the mission was until now. Our prayers are with your daughter and you. Please tell her to take care of herself and don't do what Tony did to anyone."

My mom hung up, and we all sat there in silence thinking how one night changed my life. It wasn't that he was out there bad sleeping around—he was born with it! That never crossed my mind, not one time. Once I heard him say that he was a virgin, I thought I was in the safe zone. Not! There is no such thing as a safe zone.

By the time we all got accepted into Hampton University, I was sick and getting worse every day. I refused to take all of that medication, so the disease was getting the best of me and had turned into full-blown AIDS. I joined a local church while I was in school and gave my life back to the Lord. There was no way I could make it without God. I had days of being sad, angry, and depressed. The person that gave this disease to me was dead, and I never had a chance to express the pain and hurt I was feeling. I had a lot of support from my parents and all of my homegirls. Plus, God was giving me strength to make it, but one day, I took sick, and, well … my mom has to tell you the rest.

"Lord, I'm too weak. I never thought I would outlive my daughter. One night definitely changed her life. Pretty was a bright, intelligent, beautiful young lady destined for greatness. She had so much going for herself. Somehow, she fell for one of the tricks of the Enemy. He comes to make things look good that are not good for you. He's a deceiver, a liar, and he comes to kill, steal, and destroy you. That's what he did to our daughter. He tricked her and made himself look good. But all along, his motive was to *take her life*.

"Although she gave her life to God and repented for all of her sins, and he forgave her, that didn't mean that there wouldn't be consequences behind her choices. We all know the wages of sin is death. Whenever sin is committed, something dies—be it a physical death, spiritual, or emotional. Pretty passed away two days before she was to get her bachelor's degree. Now I'm here along with her homegirls to make sure that you are aware of the many different ways the Enemy comes and of how many tricks he has up his sleeve. Which one will he use on you? Think about it!"

Romans 6:23 (New International Version)
[23]For the wages of sin is death, but the gift of God is eternal life in Christ Jesus our Lord.

A Message From the Author

The Enemy is determined to get you to a place of no return. He is no amateur at what he does; he is the master. He will use who and whatever he can to trap you. It reminds me of a fishing trip my grandmother Rether and I took many years ago. Grandma was determined to catch some fish—croppies, if I'm correct. She would set her bait and cast her line out and wait patiently for a fish to bite. After many hours—and I do mean *many* hours—she would switch her bait. She told me that the fish weren't biting what she put out at first, so she had to switch it up and change it to something she knew for sure they would come after. Finally, she caught one, and it fought hard to get off, but it was hooked and unable to get away. This is just like the Enemy. He will try over and over to trap you. He'll use a woman, man, sex, money, drugs, and many other things until he hooks you and has you thinking that there's no hope and there's no way out. Oh, but I serve a God that heals, delivers, and restores! No matter what your situation, circumstance, addiction, illness, or problem may be, God is able.

If you are tired of living a life full of sin, if you are sick in your body—depressed, stressed, confused, and don't know what to do—try God. Age doesn't matter. He's waiting with his hands open. I can assure you that God is faithful, and with him, all things are possible. He won't judge you; I promise that he will definitely love you. He'll forgive you if you ask him to. If this is something you would like to do, accept the Lord in your life and repeat this prayer, please.

Lord, I come to you admitting that I am a sinner. Lord, I need you in my life as my Lord and savior. I believe your son Jesus died on the cross and rose from the dead so that I may be saved. Lord, I surrender my all to you. Lead and guide me from this day forward, Lord. In Jesus name I pray. Amen.

I want you to know that you just made the best decision you have ever made in your life. Please feel free to contact me.

Minister LaTonia Harrell
E-mail: LaToniaHarrell@aol.com
Office: (757) 547-6970
Website: http://www.sistersbuildingsisters.com

Scriptures

1 Corinthians 6:19–20 ESV
Or do you not know that your body is a temple of the Holy Spirit within you, whom you have from God? You are not your own, for you were bought with a price. So glorify God in your body.

Romans 6:23 NIV
For the wages of sin is death, but the gift of God is eternal life in Christ Jesus our Lord.

1 Corinthians 3:16–17 ESV
Do you not know that you are God's temple and that God's Spirit dwells in you? If anyone destroys God's temple, God will destroy him. For God's temple is holy, and you are that temple.

Questions

1. What were two things Pretty did that put her life in danger?

2. Why was Pretty attracted to the young man?

3. What were two of the things that Pretty's mother always said to her?

4. Was Pretty warned about the young man in advance? If yes, who warned her and what was said to her about him?

5. What are some of the things that can take place when you have unprotected sex and sex before marriage?

6. Name two things that you allowed to take place in your life that changed your life—or could have changed your life—forever.

7. Because a man buys you gifts, does that mean he loves you? Yes or no? Why or why not?

8. Before Pretty left to meet up with the young man, what were a few things that went wrong?

9. Where did Pretty first meet the young man?

10. What was the name of the place to which the young man took Pretty?

11. What special event had taken place the day Pretty met the young man?

12. What kind of car did Pretty drive? Who bought it for her and why?

13. Why do you think Pretty gave in and had sexual intercourse with the young man in the book?

14. What were Pretty's homegirls' names?

15. Did Pretty have good friends? Yes or no? Please explain.

16. Did Pretty love herself? Yes or no? Please explain.

17. Who encouraged Pretty to go to the doctor?

18. What was the name of the young lady who warned Pretty that going out that night was a trap from the Enemy?

19. What was the name of the lady who catered the food?

20. What did the medical assistant say to Pretty about God while she was with her in the doctor's office?

21. How did Pretty feel the next day after sleeping with the young man?

22. How did the young man start to treat Pretty after they had sex?

23. What were some of the degrading names the young man called Pretty?

24. What was the young man's name?

I could go on and on with questions to make you think. My question to you is, could this have been you? Age or gender doesn't matter. The Enemy likes to play trick-or-treat with everyone. Remember, everything that looks good isn't good for you. Beware ... there's more than one way to fall into a trap! Can people live with the HIV virus? Of course they can if they are taking their medication correctly. Has anyone ever died from the HIV virus? People have died from not taking their medication properly, and it caused the virus to become full-blown AIDS. The point is that you must be wise and remember that your body doesn't belong to you! God first, self-worth, morals, and values are the keys.

Purpose

One Night Changed My Life was written to make you aware of the Enemy's "trick-or-treat" and to serve as a reminder that everything that looks good is not good for you. It doesn't matter what your temptation may be; God will always give you a choice.

Warning: One bad choice or decision can change your life forever. It's very dangerous to get caught up in the looks of someone and the material things they have, especially when you have no idea what type of person you may be dealing with. Remember, what you see isn't always what you get. The Enemy is real. He comes to steal, kill, and destroy you. He has many tricks up his sleeve. Which one will he use on you? It's time to start having self-respect, self-love, morals, and values. Never allow anyone to take you out of your character and cause you to make decisions for which only you will have to pay for the rest of your life.

Beware! It's just a matter of time before the Enemy offers you a trick or a treat.

—LaTonia Harrell

Notes

Notes

Remarks

This book is a soulful and enlightening message that will richly bless teenage and young adults desiring to be Spirit-led and made aware of the Enemy's trickery.

—La Veeta Ivory,
http://www.laveetaivory.com

This is a compelling tale of how disaster strikes when we lose focus on God, put our trust in man, and fall for the tricks of the Enemy. This story is fast paced, spirit driven, and mind blowing.

—Gina B. Flagg